Sweet Notes, Sour Notes

Sweet Notes, Sour Notes

by Nancy Smiler Levinson
illustrated by Beth Peck

LODESTAR BOOKS
Dutton   New York

Text copyright © 1993 by Nancy Smiler Levinson

Illustrations copyright © 1993 by Beth Peck

Library of Congress Cataloging-in-Publication Data
Levinson, Nancy Smiler.
  Sweet notes, sour notes / by Nancy Smiler Levinson; illustrated by Beth Peck.
    p. cm.
  "Lodestar books."
  Summary: David, growing up in the 1920s, discovers perseverance is the only way to succeed in learning to play the violin.
  ISBN 0-525-67379-2
  [1. Violin—Fiction. 2. Musicians—Fiction. 3. Perseverance (Ethics)—Fiction. 4. Jews—Fiction.] I. Peck, Beth, ill.
II. Title.
PZ7.L5794Sw   1993
[Fic]—dc20   92-19549
                                                           CIP
                                                            AC

Published in the United States by Lodestar Books,
an affiliate of Dutton Children's Books,
a division of Penguin Books USA Inc.,
375 Hudson Street, New York, New York 10014

Published simultaneously in Canada by
McClelland & Stewart, Toronto

Editor: Virginia Buckley   Designer: Richard Granald

Printed in the U.S.A.   First Edition
10 9 8 7 6 5 4 3 2 1

This book is dedicated to the
sweet memory of my grandmother,
Ida Meleck.

Contents

1

The Singing Violin

David and his grandpa stepped down from the streetcar.

"Zayde, how far is it to the concert hall?" David asked.

"A few blocks farther," David's grandpa answered. He walked tall and straight, whistling softly.

"What is it like at the concert?" David asked.

His grandpa stopped at the curb and drew his hands to his heart. "Ah, to me it is a wonder," he said.

David didn't know if the matinee concert would be a wonder to him. Once Zayde had taken David to a store to hear a symphony orchestra on a recording that spun on a phonograph machine. David liked listening to the recording, but today would be different. Now he would have to sit for a long time without moving or making a sound.

"Mischa Elman is a great violinist," Zayde told David.

"Nobody can make the violin sing like he does. Something tells me you will like the concert."

If Zayde said Mischa Elman was a great violinist, then it must be true. But David was far from sure about the rest of Zayde's words.

Soon they arrived at the concert hall. Inside the doorway Zayde removed his cap and smoothed down his bushy hair. David straightened the bow tie that was poking at his neck. They handed their tickets to a lady, and she handed them a program. David and Zayde climbed the stairs to their balcony seats.

David gazed up at the high ceiling and the glittering chandelier lights. He looked out at the red stage curtain tied back with gold braid and at the big pots of flowers on the floor in front. In the middle of the stage stood a grand piano. The concert hall was like a palace!

Finally the lights dimmed. The audience became very quiet. A lady in a long, flowing dress walked out and sat down at the piano bench.

"Who is that?" David whispered.

"She is going to accompany Mischa Elman," Zayde whispered back.

A moment later, out stepped Mischa Elman! He wore a black suit and carried a shiny violin and a long, thin bow. He stood directly in front of the piano. The audience began to applaud. Some people whistled and stomped their feet.

"He is going to start with a Beethoven sonata," Zayde

said, reading from the program. "Beethoven was one of the finest composers who ever lived."

Slowly Mischa Elman lifted the violin. He tucked one end under his chin and held the other end straight out in front of him. Then with a grand, sweeping gesture, he raised the bow and drew it across the violin strings.

Suddenly the concert hall filled with clear, sweet notes. Never had David heard such sounds. They made him think of singing birds in a tree by his house early in the morning when hardly anyone was around. But the violin music was even more beautiful. David forgot Zayde. He forgot the other people too. He felt that he was all alone with the music.

Mischa Elman played through one sonata and then began another. David was surprised that he didn't need to wriggle or run out and play as he sometimes wanted to do when sitting at his school desk. Right now he didn't even feel like moving an inch. Was there something magical about the violin?

When the concert was over, the lights went up. Mischa Elman took a deep bow, and the audience burst into loud applause. Zayde stood and shouted "Bravo!"

But David sat with his hands folded in his lap.

Zayde turned to David. "You are sitting like a statue," he said. "Why do you not applaud the great man?"

David didn't want to. Applause was too noisy right now.

Finally David said something. His voice was just above a whisper.

4

"I want to be like Mischa Elman, Zayde," he said. "I want to make the violin sing too."

Zayde drew his hands to his heart. "I had a feeling you would like the concert today," he said. "But, ah, now to hear that my grandson wants to play the violin— this is new music to my ears."

At home David found Mama, Papa, and his sister, Rose, in the kitchen. Papa was sitting at the table doing his accounts for the grocery store. Mama, in her checkered apron, was plucking a chicken to cook for supper, while at the same time she was reading a grammar book. Recently Mama had made up her mind to improve her English. Rose sat on the floor with a sketch pad on her lap. She was drawing Papa working at his arithmetic and Mama trying to do two things at once.

Sometimes Mama and Papa asked David his opinion on various matters. But this time David did not wait to be asked his opinion of the concert. Immediately he began to tell his family all about the matinee performance from beginning to end.

When he finished, he took a deep breath. Then he announced, "I want to have a violin."

What would Mama and Papa say to that? he wondered. He stood back and waited. But Mama and Papa did not say anything. They only glanced at each other. Rose, on the other hand, snickered, and very loudly too.

David sat down next to Papa.

5

"Papa, can I?" he asked. "Please? Can I have a violin?"

"Last week you said you were going to become a fireman," Papa reminded him. "The week before you said you wanted to become president of the United States."

"So, what'll it be next week?" Mama asked.

"Oh, Mama," David said. "I'll never change my mind again. It's the violin I'll want forever."

"You're too young to use the word 'forever,'" said Mama.

Papa removed his eyeglasses. "Profits at the grocery aren't so high this year," he said. "Maybe you'll play the violin once and then put it in the closet. That would be like throwing money away."

"Oh no, Papa," David pleaded. "I'll only put the violin in the closet when I'm sleeping. I'll play it all the time when I'm awake. How else can I become a great violinist?"

"*Great?*" said Mama. "Papa and I don't expect great. Whatever you do, *good* is fine with us."

Papa put his eyeglasses on again. "We'll see," he said. "We'll see."

2

Daydreaming

One minute David stared into the inkwell on his desk. The next minute he stared at the portrait of George Washington hanging in the fourth-grade classroom. How could he listen to the teacher? How could he pay attention to the geography lesson? The melodies of the concert music were singing too loudly inside his head.

All of a sudden David heard his name called. "David Raskin?"

It was the teacher, Miss Bamberger.

"David, the class is waiting," Miss Bamberger said. "Can you answer the question? What are North America's most important inland waterways?"

David felt his neck and cheeks turn warm.

Everyone in the room shifted to watch him. The whole class was waiting to see what he would do. But he couldn't do anything. He couldn't answer any part of the question.

Finally the class looked back at Miss Bamberger at the front blackboard. Everyone waited to see what would happen next. Would Miss Bamberger mete out a punishment to David Raskin?

Miss Bamberger glared at David. "Were you daydreaming?" she asked.

David nodded.

"I will have to give you a demerit," said Miss Bamberger. "Maybe next time you will think twice before you start to daydream."

"Yes, Miss Bamberger," David said.

Miss Bamberger went on with the geography lesson. She tapped her pointer stick on the map of the United States.

"The important inland waterways are the five Great Lakes," she said. "Arnold Zuckerman, can you name and locate those lakes for us? You may use my pointer stick if you like."

Arnie was David's good friend. David glanced in his direction to see what would happen to *him*. Arnie sat up straight. He looked ready to answer. But he didn't say anything right away. First he took a big gulp and then a hurried swallow.

Aha! The class had another troublemaker! David was glad he was not the only one.

Miss Bamberger glared at Arnie.

"Are you chewing gum in school?" she asked angrily.

"No, ma'am," Arnie answered. He opened his mouth wide to prove that it was empty.

The class burst into laughter.

Miss Bamberger did not try to call for order. She marched down the aisle to Arnie's seat, bent forward, and gazed right into his mouth.

"Well," she huffed. "There's no gum in there now. But I know your trick, Arnold Zuckerman. That will be double demerits."

"Yes, ma'am," Arnie said.

David admired Arnie's ability to keep a straight face after swallowing a wad of chewing gum and telling a big lie.

At last the dismissal bell rang. All the pupils lined up and left the room. They were extra quiet and orderly today. Nobody else wanted a demerit from the teacher.

David and Arnie tried to be quiet and orderly, too, when they left, but it was hard to hold back their snickering. As soon as they reached the schoolyard, they broke into a run and laughed until they were nearly out of breath. When they got to the parkway, they slowed down and walked arm-in-arm.

"What were you daydreaming about?" Arnie asked David.

David wasn't sure that he could explain to Arnie, or to anyone for that matter. But he owed his friend a try.

"Well . . ." David began, "my grandpa took me to a concert—in the biggest place I've ever seen. And there was a great violinist who stood in the middle of the stage and . . ." David paused, picturing the concert stage. Then he went on. "The musician's name was Mischa

10

Elman, and when he played his violin, I had a feeling inside that I never felt before."

"What kind of feeling was it?" Arnie asked.

"I don't know," David said. "It was just different. When Miss Bamberger called on me, I was thinking about the music I had heard. I was imagining that I was playing music like that too."

"You want to play a *fiddle?*" Arnie exclaimed. "Ya hoo! Yippie!" He slapped his knee and whooped in a circle like a square-dancing cowboy the boys had read about in an adventure story.

"No, a violin," said David.

"Oh." Arnie shrugged. "I thought you meant a fiddle."

"No," David said, shaking his head. He was disappointed. He had hoped that Arnie would say his daydream was something special.

They walked a little farther.

"Want to find some kids and play kick-the-can?" Arnie asked.

"No thanks," David answered.

"How about marbles?" Arnie suggested. "I traded my moonstone for a new aggie. If you win it, we can play for keeps."

"Not today," said David. "I want to go to Papa's grocery."

Last winter Papa had bought David a softball for Chanukah. But Papa hid it on a shelf behind the soap powder boxes until the first night of the holiday. It was

11

not a holiday time now, but David hoped that today Papa was hiding a violin.

"Your papa never lets us play at the store," Arnie said. "He only puts a broom in our hands and makes us sweep."

"I know, but I want to go to Papa's grocery," said David. He did not try to explain anything more to Arnie. Besides, Arnie had called the violin a fiddle.

3

The Search

At the grocery Papa was hunched inside the front window stacking oatmeal boxes in a pyramid display.

"How was your day at school, boys?" he asked over his shoulder.

"It was swell, Mr. Raskin," Arnie answered. "We learned about the Great Lakes. Did you know they are North America's most important inland waterways?"

"You don't say," said Papa.

David remained quiet and allowed Arnie to speak. That way he wouldn't have to tell Papa anything about the demerits Miss Bamberger had put in her book.

Papa stepped out of the window. He stood back and admired his display. Then he reached for the push broom.

"All day you used your brains," he said to the boys. "Now you can use your muscles." He smiled and handed them the broom.

Arnie stepped back and let the broom handle fall to David. David put his reader and spelling book on the counter. The counter was already crowded with tins, a coffee grinder, and a small scale.

David began to sweep up and down the narrow aisles. Arnie followed.

"See? What did I tell you?" Arnie whispered to David.

David ignored Arnie and went on sweeping. After every step he stopped to peek behind the goods on the shelves. He found a wet napkin and a few dead flies, but he didn't find anything resembling a violin.

Arnie continued to follow David as he swept the pile of dirt out the door, across the sidewalk, and over the curb.

"David?" Arnie asked.

"What, Arnie?"

"I like playing marbles better than watching you sweep," he said. "I even like geography better. Good-bye."

David didn't run after Arnie. Today he had something too important on his mind. He could play marbles with Arnie another time.

Papa finished helping a lady customer. Then he took the broom from David.

"Thank you for helping, David," he said.

The lady pinched David's cheek and patted her hand over the pinch.

"You have a good son, Mr. Raskin," she told David's

papa. "Someday he'll be working side by side with you. Then you'll stand tall with pride."

Papa thanked the lady for the compliment and handed David his reader and spelling book.

"All right, you can go home now," Papa told David. "Tell Mama I'll try to lock up on time tonight."

David hurried out. Papa had told him to go home. Maybe that was a hint. Maybe the surprise was waiting for him there.

When David rushed into the front room, he startled Mama so that she accidentally pricked her finger with a sewing needle. She was trimming a hat with a cluster of artificial flowers, while at the same time a book lay open on her lap.

"Mama!" David exclaimed. "Is there something here for me?"

"The hat is for Rose," Mama said. "I'm making it over from last year."

"Is there something else?"

"A glass of fresh milk."

David sighed. "Is that all?" he asked.

Mama looked puzzled.

After he came home from the concert, David had asked about getting a violin, and he had asked again that night at bedtime. But it seemed that neither Mama nor Papa had heard a word.

4

Pickles in a Jar

It was Sunday morning. All week David had been thinking about discussing the violin with Zayde today. David knew his grandpa would help him.

Right after breakfast David made an announcement. "I'm going to walk to Zayde's apartment now."

Rose jumped up from the table.

"I'm coming too," she added. "Ooooh, and I'm going to bring Zayde a beautiful watercolor I made."

David lowered his eyes. "I don't have a present to bring," he said.

"I made chicken soup with farfel," said Mama cheerfully. "There's a jar for Zayde in the icebox."

"But *I* didn't make it," David said.

"Don't worry," Papa told him. "Zayde will love you just the same."

Mama packed the jar in a paper bag and handed it to David. Then David set out. Just like Rose said, she came along too. All the way up the street she chattered about this and she chattered about that. If David's arms weren't full with the soup jar, he would have covered his ears against her endless talk.

"Queenie is having a birthday party this afternoon," Rose said. "It's going to be all in pink. Queenie has a pink dress with a sash, and pink stockings. There will be cake with pink icing and strawberry flavor ice cream. That's pink too."

David only wished that Rose were at the pink party right now.

"Queenie is going to let me give out the prizes," said Rose. "I was the first person she invited."

David quickened his step.

A few minutes later they approached a lady pushing a baby buggy. Rose stopped to peer inside.

"What a little darling!" Rose cried. Then she reached into the buggy to kootchy-coo the baby. "Ooooh, what tiny fingers it has. What an itsy-bitsy nose."

David was just a little curious to see what was bundled up inside the blankets. He peeked quickly inside the baby buggy. But he did not kootchy-coo. He didn't want to do anything that Rose did, and besides, the baby was sleeping and didn't look very exciting anyway.

Soon David and Rose arrived at Zayde's small, corner building. Zayde's apartment was on the first floor in the middle of the hall. David and Rose raced to his door to knock first. But Zayde was already standing at the open door waiting for them.

"How do you always know we are here before we knock?" David asked.

"The little bird in my cuckoo clock tells me so." Zayde laughed.

Zayde gave David and Rose a tight hug. David liked the familiar, gentle scratch of his whiskers and the smell of his soap.

"I brought you a present, Zayde," Rose said. She handed her watercolor to him.

"Such an artwork!" said Zayde, opening his eyes wide. "This is more beautiful than the last."

Rose grinned. "I think so too."

David removed the jar of soup from the paper bag and held it out. There was nothing beautiful about it at all. He hadn't made any part of it. He hadn't even stirred it once while it was simmering on the stove.

"David, how did you know I dreamed of chicken soup last night?" Zayde asked.

Just then the door of the cuckoo clock on the wall sprung open, and out popped the little bird to chirp the hour.

"Now I know." Zayde laughed. "The cuckoo bird must have visited your house and told you." Zayde put the soup and the watercolor side by side on the table.

"Come. See something I made," he said. He pointed to a row of jars on top of the kitchen cupboard. "Once these were small cucumbers, but I soaked them in vinegar and pickling salt. Then I waited seven weeks. And

now they are the best sour pickles you could find any-where."

Zayde opened a jar, pulled out a pickle, and offered David and Rose a taste. Rose stepped back, but David accepted the offer and took a small bite. It was so sour it sent a shiver up his spine and stung his nose. Never-theless, it tasted good.

Zayde took a bite, too, and smacked his lips. "Now that's a pickle!" he exclaimed. "You are not interested in trying my fine pickles, Rose?"

"I would like one," explained Rose, "but I don't like anything sour."

"Then you would not like my pickles." Zayde laughed gently and winked at David. David also understood Rose's nonsense.

"That's not one bit nice to laugh at me," Rose said, sticking her nose up and turning away. "I'm going into the front room to hang my watercolor. I have to find just the right spot."

David was glad Rose had left the room. Now he could talk to Zayde alone.

"Zayde," he began. "Mischa Elman and his music fol-low me wherever I go. Sometimes he walks with me, and sometimes he visits when I am lying in bed at night. He even sits with me in school and gets me in trouble."

"You are telling the truth about such a visitor?" Zayde asked.

"Yes, Zayde." David nodded.

"Not even my little cuckoo bird had an idea that you

would have such special feelings about the violin, David," said Zayde.

David went on. "Every time I ask Mama and Papa for a violin, the only thing they say is 'we'll see.' "

Zayde smiled warmly. "Don't worry about Mama and Papa," he said. "I'll talk to them."

5

Something Oddly Shaped

David lived in a two-family house. That was a building with two houses attached side by side.

David hurried up the block to his house. He clutched the cigar box that contained his collection of bottle caps. He and Arnie had been trading for keeps. David ran up the walk. His bottle caps shook inside the cigar box.

When he looked up, he saw Mama at the window holding back the lace curtain. She waved to him.

David went inside. The whole family was in the front room. Papa, Mama, and Zayde stood grinning. Even Rose wore a smile on her face.

"We've been waiting for you," Mama said eagerly.

"Do you have some news?" David asked.

"Here is the news," Papa said, and he handed David an oddly shaped case with a handle. "We rented this for fifty cents a month," he added. "That way, if it goes in

23

the closet, we can take it back. We won't be throwing good money away."

David took hold of the oddly shaped case. He knew instantly what it was!

"A violin!" he exclaimed. "It's really a violin."

He could hardly wait to play it. At once he opened the case and gazed inside. Just looking at the polished musical instrument made his heart beat fast. Everyone was watching him and waiting to see what he would do.

David lifted the violin. He tucked one end under his chin and held the other out straight in front of him. Then with a grand, sweeping gesture, he raised the bow and drew it across the violin strings.

Screech! Squeak! Squawk! What awful, terrible noises!

Mama and Papa made a face, and Rose clamped her hands over her ears.

"Ooooh, what sour notes!" Rose exclaimed. "Just like Zayde's pickles."

David looked down, embarrassed. How did Mischa Elman make it look so easy?

Zayde smiled gently and lifted David's chin in his hand. "Don't feel bad," he said. "You are a beginner. And the beginning is a good place to start."

David tried to smile too, but he couldn't. He pictured the concert hall with its glittering chandelier lights. He pictured the red curtain and the pots of flowers in front of it. He heard Mischa Elman's music and the burst of applause from the audience.

"I wish I could make one good sound right now," David said. He put down the violin and the bow and shoved his hands deep inside his pockets.

"Mischa Elman took music lessons first," Zayde told David. "And so will you."

6

Plinks and Plucks

The next afternoon David and Zayde walked to the streetcar stop. Zayde whistled softly as he flipped his nickel streetcar fare high into the air and caught it in his hand. David carried his rented violin case at his side and tried not to let it bump against his knee.

When the streetcar arrived, they climbed aboard and paid the conductor. Then they rode to Twelfth Avenue, where the violin teacher lived in a narrow, brick house. In the front yard there was a small garden.

Zayde rang the doorbell. David heard the strike of chimes coming from inside. What else awaited him behind that door? he wondered. His hands felt cold and damp.

Suddenly the door flung open. There stood a lady with hair rolled on top of her head in a corkscrew that tilted to one side. She wore long, sparkling earrings that swung back and forth when she moved.

"Come in," she said in a low voice. "You are right on time. I have just finished preparing a lecture on opera to give at my next ladies' music and garden club meeting."

David followed Zayde inside.

"Let me introduce you to Madame Markov," Zayde said to David.

"So. This is your grandson," Madame Markov said.

"Hello," said David in a soft voice. He knew it was not polite to stare at people, but he couldn't help staring at her.

"Let me see your hands," said Madame Markov to David, taking his case from him and then grabbing both his hands. She studied them carefully at close range. Was she going to tell him that his hands were dirty? he wondered. Would she embarrass him by sending him to her bathroom to wash? But she said nothing about dirt. "The fingers are good for the instrument," she remarked instead. "The hands . . . they will grow strong in time." David was glad to hear this remark.

Madame Markov led Zayde and David into the parlor. The smell of perfume filled the air. The room gave off a soft, red glow from a lamp with a red shade. On a table stood the framed picture of a man with white hair that stuck out in spikes. The man did not look very happy. He must be Madame Markov's husband, David thought.

Zayde offered to spend the hour outside in the garden. He said that way he wouldn't interfere with the lesson.

David wanted Zayde to stay with him, but he did not dare speak. The red glow from the lamp seemed to grow brighter.

"Come, my young pupil," said Madame Markov, inviting David to sit beside her on the sofa. She took David's violin and laid it across her lap.

"The violin is like a box," she said. "When we vibrate the strings, the sounds come from these air holes." Delicately with one finger she plucked at each of the four strings. "The strings are stretched and tuned to sound different notes," she told him. "Yes?"

David nodded.

Her finger plinking the strings made quick, interesting sounds, but not the ones that David wanted to hear. Finally he worked up the courage to speak.

"How do you make the sounds last longer?" he asked.

"Then you do not pluck," she said. "You use the bow to play legato." Madame Markov stood up and demonstrated with the bow so that the legato vibrations rang out and floated all about them. She played for several minutes, sometimes with her eyes closed. When she stopped, she sighed deeply. "Such music is glorious, yes?" she asked.

"Oh, yes," David answered.

Next Madame Markov showed David how to hold the violin. She showed him how to curl his fingers around the violin neck and how to move the bow flat across the strings. Then she taught him the notes of the musical scale: *do, re, mi, fa, sol, la, ti, do.*

David worked at keeping his elbow bent just the way he was shown. And he worked at holding his hand the right way to keep his fingers curled on the fingerboard, the black part of the violin neck. This was necessary so he could press down on the strings to change the pitch of the notes. All of this was new and hard enough. But hardest of all was finding the exact position of the notes on the strings. Finding the places where those notes were located was not like searching on the schoolroom map of the United States, where you could see everything in its proper place.

"So," Madame Markov said. David listened eagerly for what he was going to learn next.

"So," she said again. "Now your first lesson is finished."

"But how can I learn to find the notes on the strings?" David asked.

"You will learn in time," said Madame Markov.

"When can I learn to read notes from music books?" David asked.

"In time," said Madame Markov. "You cannot learn everything at once. For now, you must go home and practice, practice, practice."

7

Practice, Practice, Practice

David stood in the bedroom he shared with Rose. Rose was not home, so it was a good time to practice. Yesterday when he had been practicing, she kept coming in and interrupting him.

Now David pressed his fingers on the fingerboard and drew the bow across one of the strings. The sound he made was not a screech. It was a clear sound, and it made him feel good to hear it. But it was not the note that he was searching for. David moved his fingers to a different spot and tried again. That was not the correct note either. He was good at hearing what was right and what was wrong, but he still could not find the notes quickly without making mistakes first.

If he did not hurry up and find the notes right away, how could he learn to play a song? How could he ever stand on the stage of a grand concert hall? It would take years, he thought. Even forever. Maybe he was better off playing marbles.

Suddenly there was a knock at the front door. What a good sound *that* was!

David ran to the door and opened it.

"Arnie, old pal!" David exclaimed.

Arnie held out a football.

"Want to come out and have a catch?" he asked.

"I sure do!" said David.

Just then David's mama appeared.

"Hello, Arnie," she said.

"Hello, Mrs. Raskin," said Arnie. "David and I are going outside to have a catch."

Mama looked at David.

"I thought you were going to practice," she said.

"I finished," said David.

Mama looked at the clock.

"In my opinion, five minutes is a short practice time," she said.

"My arm is so tired," said David. "My neck is stiff too."

Mama looked at Arnie's football.

"Is having a catch the way to rest an arm?" Mama asked.

David didn't know how to answer that question.

"I'm going to practice later," David said. "I'm going to practice the scale like Madame Markov showed me. Then I'm going to practice long and short notes. And after that I'm going to practice fast and slow notes."

"That's good," said Mama. "Papa will be glad to hear it. He'll be glad to know the violin is not in the closet already."

"Oh, no! That will never happen, Mama," David said. "I can promise you that."

David put on his coat and ran outside to play.

8

The Duet

David sat in his room looking at the violin. The violin was lying in its case. The bow was in the case too. David thought about the exercises he was supposed to practice. They were the same old exercises he had to play over and over. He felt his sore arm and stiff neck. He imagined Arnie winning more and more marbles and bottle caps than he could ever dream of.

But a promise was a promise.

David had a new arrangement for practicing now. It was Zayde's idea, and Mama and Papa had agreed. David was allowed to practice for half an hour in the bedroom with the door closed. He was to have quiet and privacy, and during that time Rose was forbidden to go into the room. If she needed anything, she had to get it before or wait until afterward.

Every day Rose argued about the arrangement. Mama

said that by the time Rose finished arguing, a half hour was gone already.

David stretched his fingers for several minutes. Then he shook out his arms, one at a time. Then he turned the pages of his exercise book.

Finally he picked up the violin and put his chin on the chin rest. He lifted the bow to begin Exercise Number One. It was the *do, re, mi* scale. He had learned to read notes on the music page, and now Madame Markov called the notes by letters instead of *do, re, mi*. Exercise Number One was playing the scale in C major.

C, D, E, David played up the scale. *F, G, A, B, C.*

Then he played down the scale. *C, B, A, G, F, E, D, C.*

The violin still squawked plenty, but it didn't screech and squawk quite as much as it used to.

Just then Rose swung open the door and stuck her head inside.

"What's that noise supposed to be?" she asked.

"It's none of your business," David scowled. "And you're not supposed to be bothering me."

"Queenie and I have to get something," Rose said.

Queenie peeked over Rose's shoulder. They both snickered.

"Why didn't you get it before?" David asked.

"Because we didn't know we wanted it before," Rose answered. "Did we, Queenie?"

"No," Queenie said. "We just decided to get it."

"It's the creamer and pitcher to my china tea set," said Rose. "It's very important."

Together Rose and Queenie swept into the room and began poking everywhere. They rummaged through dresser drawers, opened the window, and, for one last good measure, jumped on the beds. David grabbed Rose's stuffed Lamby Doll with the bell around its neck and threw it at her. Finally Rose and Queenie raced out.

David slammed the door behind them. He marched back and forth angrily. Violin practice was turning out to be a real problem. It was ruining his whole life! He began to wish that he had never started in the first place.

But a promise was a promise. How could he go back on his word now? What would Zayde and Papa and Mama say to him?

David sighed. He stretched his fingers. He shook out his arms. At last he picked up the violin and began again. He was just playing a long middle *C* note when suddenly he heard a high screeching sound accompanying him. David looked around. He didn't see anything. He went back to his violin and played a long *D* note. There was the frantic-sounding screech again. "Ye-ooow!"

David turned once more. This time he saw the problem. It was Ginger, Queenie's big old yellow cat, on the window ledge. And outside the window, David heard Rose and Queenie laughing.

David leaped toward the window and shouted out at them.

The frightened cat sprang off the ledge into the room.

Mama heard the commotion and came running.

"What's going on?" she asked. Then she saw the cat.

"Rose and Queenie did it," David said. He was glad he was tattling. They deserved to be tattled on.

"Oh dear, oh, my," Mama said, shaking her head, and she ordered the girls inside at once. They weren't snickering anymore.

"What kind of nonsense is going on?" Mama asked them, standing with her hands firmly on her hips.

"David's noise and Ginger's meowing sound the same. We wanted them to perform a duet," Rose said.

"In my opinion, that is shameful," said Mama. "And in Papa's opinion, it's shameful too."

"I'm sorry," Queenie said. She picked up her cat and left to go home.

"Rose," said Mama, "what do *you* have to say to David?"

"I'm sorry too," Rose said, but David didn't think she really meant it.

"Close the window, Rose," Mama ordered. "And come into the kitchen this minute. Papa is bringing Zayde home for Sabbath dinner. You can set the table, peel the potatoes, scrape the carrots, and wash the greens. And when you are done with all of that, you can do David's job too—polish the candlesticks."

"Yes, Mama," said Rose.

David sat on the edge of the bed, holding the violin across his lap. He didn't feel like working on Exercise Number One anymore. He didn't feel like working on any exercise. He was furious with Rose. But she was

right. Most of the time all he could do was make a noise like a screeching cat.

Slowly David put the violin and bow back into the case. Then he carried the case across the room and stood in front of his closet door. He stood for a long time, staring and thinking.

It was a good thing the violin was only rented, he thought. Papa and Mama couldn't accuse him of wasting good money.

But they would have something else to say to him instead.

"We told you so," they would say. "We told you that you would change your mind."

Worst of all, they would never believe him again.

As David stood thinking, beautiful concert music began to sing inside his head. Glorious music, as Madame Markov had called it. How he wished he could make such music come from his violin right now! Just the way he heard it. But he couldn't. It was too bad. David opened his closet door and put the violin inside.

9

A Little Story

Everyone was seated at the Sabbath dinner table. Mama lit the Sabbath candles and recited the blessing over them, first in Hebrew and afterward in English.

"May these Sabbath candles bring light to all who behold them," she said. "And may we be granted Sabbath joy and peace."

Papa gave the blessing over the wine, and Zayde gave the blessing over the loaf of challah.

Dinner was served. David ladled a large matzo ball into each bowl of soup. Rose passed around the platter of roast beef and vegetables. She made sure she let everyone know that she had peeled the potatoes and scraped the carrots and washed the greens.

Papa and Zayde paid a compliment to both cooks.

"This is a dinner fit for kings and queens," said Zayde.

Papa asked Rose about her day at school.

"It was fine, Papa," Rose answered. "We had long division and a talk on proper teeth care."

"Hmmmm," said Papa. "And how was your day, David?"

"Miss Bamberger is reading us an adventure story about a boy named Tom Sawyer," David said. "Tom and his friend Huck are always getting into some kind of mischief."

"Hmmmm," said Papa. "And how are you and the violin getting along?"

David almost choked on a piece of challah. This was not a good time to tell Papa where he had put the violin. He did not know when would be a good time to tell Papa. David continued chewing.

All of a sudden Rose grinned and said, "Oh, Papa! David is playing splendidly."

"Is that so?" Papa asked, looking up at Mama suspiciously.

Mama remained quiet and wiped the corners of her mouth with her napkin. David understood that no one was going to tattle on Rose to Papa. It seemed that Rose had already learned her lesson today.

After dinner David took Zayde aside.

"Zayde, I have something to tell you," David said. "Rose doesn't really think I play splendidly. She's only teasing. She's only being mean."

Zayde rubbed his whiskers.

"I'm no good at all," David said. "I'll never be able to make the violin sing."

"Let me tell you a little story," Zayde began. "Many years ago in the old country, musicians traveled from village to village. How I loved to listen to them! How I wanted to be a musician too! When we came to America, I wanted to play the violin. But we were poor. I had to go to work in a sewing factory. I had no chance for music lessons. All day I had to listen to the noise of factory machines instead."

David looked up at Zayde. There were tears in his grandpa's eyes as Zayde told his little story. But it wasn't such a little story at all.

"You are lucky you have a chance to learn," Zayde told David. "You have a special feeling for the violin. And a good ear. If you do not learn, you will miss making the violin sing. Other people will miss hearing you too."

David went to his room and removed the violin from his closet. Maybe he could try again. Maybe he could at least learn to play one little song.

10

The Nickel Fare

Finally the long-awaited day arrived. David was ready. Madame Markov was going to teach him how to play his first song. It was called "Twinkle, Twinkle, Little Star," and it was written by a composer named Mozart.

But Zayde couldn't take David to his lesson today. He was busy paying a visit to the doctor. Zayde had arranged to come at the end of the lesson to take David home.

So Mama gave David a nickel fare to ride the streetcar by himself. She trusted him because he had gone with Zayde many times before. David knew what number streetcar to get on. He knew when to pull the cord to get off. He knew which way to walk to Madame Markov's house.

David hurried down the street and crossed through the park. The streetcar stop was one block farther. He car-

ried his violin case in one hand and the nickel fare in the other.

He began to whistle like Zayde did, and he flipped the nickel high into the air the same way too. But the nickel didn't land in his hand. It hit the curb and rolled along the gutter. Before David could catch it, the nickel rolled onto an open grating and dropped down into a drain.

David stooped forward on his hands and knees and pressed his face against the grating. There was his nickel. It lay at the bottom of the drain next to a small pool of water. Only a miracle could help him get it out. He could hardly think what to do.

Papa would say that David must learn a lesson when it came to the important matter of money. Mama and Papa would refuse to give him another nickel.

He could set out walking to Madame Markov's. But what if he did not get there in time for the lesson? What if Madame Markov was so angry she told him never to come back? Then what would he tell Zayde? It would be all David's fault if he missed his chance to learn the violin.

Once more David gazed down at the nickel. What could reach it? he wondered. The long, thin bow. That might work. David took the bow out of the case and poked it down into the drain as far as it would go. It reached the bottom all right, but how could he get the nickel out?

Maybe he could put something sticky on the end. Then he could press it onto the nickel and pull it up. A wad of chewing gum! That was what he needed! Arnie lived on the other side of the park. He would probably have a wet, gummy wad all ready.

David ran without stopping to Arnie's house. He banged on the door until Arnie opened it. David told him what had happened and how he hoped to get his nickel back.

"I stuck a wad of gum under the kitchen table before dinner last night," Arnie said. "I'll get it."

David waited. The minute hand on the kitchen clock ticked away.

"Here it is," said Arnie, reappearing. "But it's hard as a stone."

"Oh," David said. He stood silently for a minute. "I guess my idea won't work after all."

"Sorry," said Arnie.

"Thanks anyway," David said.

"What are you going to do?" Arnie asked.

"I guess I'll have to walk," David answered.

"You'll be late," said Arnie. "Does Madame Markov give demerits?"

"I don't know," David answered. He blinked back tears and set off.

Block after block he followed the streetcar tracks. It grew colder, and he shivered. Once he stopped to pull his mittens out of his pockets and put them on his icy hands. Another time he stopped to pull his cap down tighter over his ears.

Finally he recognized Madame Markov's street. He

hurried his last steps to her house. He had no idea how much time had passed.

David rang the doorbell. Madame Markov flung open the door. "So!" she said. "You are not a serious pupil after all!"

"Oh, I am! You have to believe me!" David pleaded. "I've practiced my exercises over and over. I'm ready to learn a song."

"Do you call a boy who comes when the lesson time is over a serious pupil!" Madame Markov cried.

David tried to explain what had happened, but she stormed into the parlor.

"Oh, please, Madame Markov," David begged.

Madame Markov snatched up the framed picture of the man with the hair that stood up in spikes. "Do you hear that, Ludwig?" she asked the photograph. "Do you believe what this boy says?"

"Oh, I know your husband believes me," David burst out. "I just know it!"

"My husband!" Madame Markov roared with laughter. "Oh, my eager young pupil. This is not my husband. This is the great composer Ludwig van Beethoven. He has been dead for nearly one hundred years." She put the picture back on the table and roared with laughter again.

David laughed, too, at his foolish mistake.

Madame Markov sighed deeply and threw her hands upward.

"How can I refuse a boy who thinks I am the wife of

49

Ludwig van Beethoven?" she said. She was no longer speaking to the picture, and she was no longer speaking directly to David. It seemed she was speaking to no one in particular. But she didn't look quite so angry with him anymore.

"But what about . . . ?" David began.

"Yes. What about your lesson?" Madame Markov said. "It is impossible now. You have missed it today. *Pffft!* It is over! But there is next time. Next time you will put your nickel fare inside your hand and put your hand inside your mitten. Then the nickel will not roll into a drain. You won't have to run to your friend's house for chewing gum. And you won't have to walk all the way to Madame Markov's."

"Yes, Madame Markov," David said. The red light in the room glowed warmly. How glad he was to have another chance to try. Now *he* would have a little story to tell Zayde. He knew Zayde would understand.

11

The Beautiful Present

C, C, G, G, A, A, G, Rest. F, F, E, E, D, D, C, Rest. Sometimes there was still a screech, and sometimes there was a squawk. But "Twinkle, Twinkle, Little Star" was starting to sound like "Twinkle, Twinkle, Little Star." Practicing a song was hard work too, but it was more fun than exercises.

David was so busy practicing that he didn't hear the front door open and close.

Mama and Rose came rushing inside. They were covered with tiny, soft snowflakes.

Mama looked worried. "We have some news," she said. "Zayde isn't feeling well."

This news filled David with worry too.

"The doctor paid a call to Zayde," said Mama. "He said it is not serious, but he put Zayde to bed to rest."

David was glad it was not serious. Still, he didn't like to think of Zayde sick in bed.

"I'm going to visit him right away," David said.

"That would make him feel better," agreed Mama. "But in my opinion, a short visit would be best. The doctor said he must not get too tired."

"I won't stay long," David said.

He put on his coat and cap.

"I'm going to bake Zayde a delicious poppy seed cake," Rose said. "That will really cheer him up."

David tried to think of something he could bring. What could it be? he wondered. All of a sudden an idea came to him! What a wonderful surprise he had for Zayde! He snatched his violin and bow, put them into the case, and snapped the case shut. Then he hurried out into the new-fallen snow.

When he arrived at the apartment, David went right into Zayde's bedroom. Zayde was sitting up in bed. On the bedside table there stood a bottle of medicine and a jar of sour pickles.

Zayde smiled at the sight of David.

"I knew you would come to visit." He laughed. "A little cuckoo bird told me so."

"How are you feeling now?" David asked.

"Not so bad," answered Zayde. "The doctor said I will be fine if I don't shovel the snow or dance on the ceiling."

David laughed. Then he said, "Zayde, I brought a present for you."

"Oh? What could that be?" Zayde asked.

"It isn't a watercolor," answered David, "and it isn't a poppy seed cake."

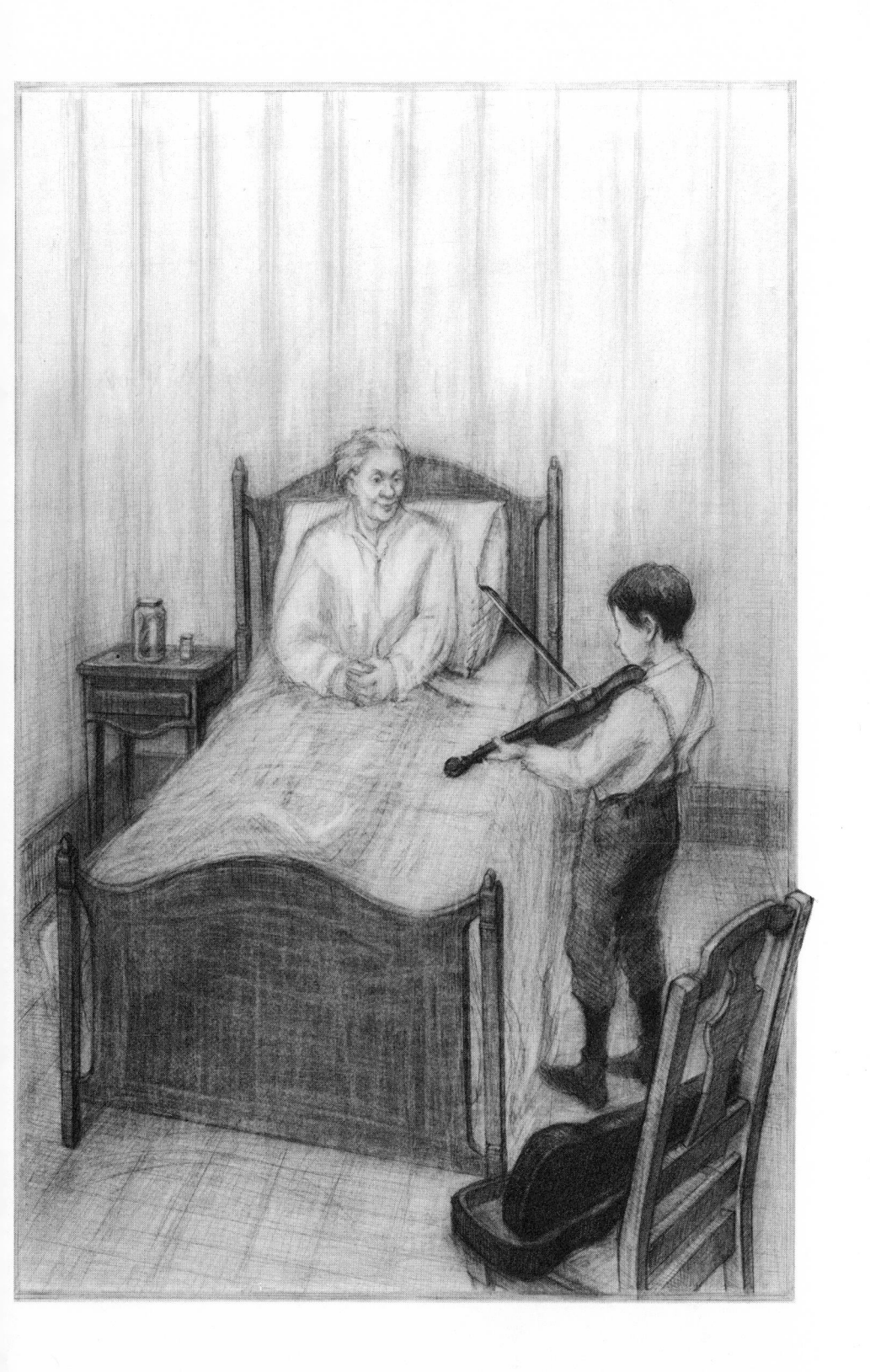

"Then what is it?" Zayde asked.

"It's a song," David said.

"A song?" Zayde asked. "You are bringing a song all the way up the street, down the apartment hall, and into my room?"

"Yes," said David.

David removed his coat and cap. He lifted the violin from the case. He took his position at the foot of the bed. Then slowly he drew the bow across the strings and began.

"Twinkle, Twinkle, Little Star" rang out loud and clear.

Zayde's eyes grew bright. He sat up very straight. His foot wiggled back and forth under the blanket, keeping time with the music.

When the song was finished, David took a deep bow, and Zayde burst into applause.

"Ah, what sweet notes you have played for me!" Zayde exclaimed. "You have given me the most beautiful present I ever had!"

David smiled proudly. What a wonder he felt in his heart!

About the Author

NANCY SMILER LEVINSON is an award-winning author, lecturer, and former editor. Her most recent book for Lodestar was *Christopher Columbus: Voyager to the Unknown*. About *Sweet Notes, Sour Notes* she says: "It comes from recollections of my grandparents and of my family's deep appreciation of music."

Ms. Levinson and her husband are the parents of two sons and live in southern California.

About the Illustrator

BETH PECK is a children's book illustrator. Recent books that she has illustrated are *A Christmas Memory* by Truman Capote and *The Snow Goose* by Paul Gallico for Knopf, and *Matthew and Tilly* by Rebecca C. Jones for Dutton. She lives in Menomonie, Wisconsin, with her husband and young daughter.